P9-CRW-296

ABSOLUTELY Alfie

and the

WORST BEST SLEEPOVER

Books about Absolutely Alfie

❋ ❋ ❋

BOOK #1

Absolutely Alfie and the Furry Purry Secret

BOOK #2

Absolutely Alfie and the First Week Friends

BOOK #3

Absolutely Alfie and the Worst Best Sleepover

ABSOLUTELY Alfie

and the

WORST BEST SLEEPOVER

SALLY WARNER

illustrated by SHEARRY MALONE

VIKING

VIKING
An imprint of Penguin Random House LLC
375 Hudson Street
New York, New York 10014

First published in the United States of America by Viking,
an imprint of Penguin Random House LLC, 2018

LIBRARY OF CONGRESS CATALOGING-IN-PUBLICATION DATA IS AVAILABLE
HC ISBN: 9781101999929
PB ISBN: 9781101999943

Printed in U.S.A.

1 3 5 7 9 10 8 6 4 2

To my youngest new friend, Edie Chambers.

—S.W.

To Lauren—

My favorite bookworm, longtime friend,

and supporter. This one's for you.

—S.M.

* * *

Contents

ABSOLUTELY Alfie

and the

WORST BEST SLEEPOVER

Freeze!

"I finished that worksheet," seven-year-old Alfie Jakes told her big brother EllRay on Monday morning, after a drippy bite of cereal. "But I think weekend homework is just mean. *Mr. Havens* is mean."

She was kidding. Mr. Havens was Alfie's second grade teacher. His nickname was "Coach," because he taught basketball during recess and after school. All the kids in Alfie's class liked him—even if they didn't like his homework assignments.

Weekend homework least of all.

It was the fourth week of school, just past the middle of September. Alfie and eleven-year-old

EllRay were eating as fast as they could. Their mom was packing snacks and lunches for the day at the kitchen island.

"You know he's not mean," EllRay said. "And if you think that homework was bad, wait until sixth grade," he added, making a face.

"I *have* to wait, don't I?" Alfie asked. "Because I'm only in second grade now. So *duh*."

Alfie and EllRay liked to tease each other, but they knew they were a team—and their gray kitten, Princess, was the mascot.

"Was the worksheet hard?" EllRay asked, looking up from the back of the cereal box he was reading.

"It was no big deal," Alfie said, shrugging. "It was easy as pie, in fact."

"Easy as pie?" EllRay asked, grinning. "What kind of pie? Rock pie? Cement pie? Because you were griping about it like crazy last night."

"Not because it was hard," Alfie said, scooping up another bite of cereal. "I just don't know that much about the boys in my class, that's all. Why should I? Or even some of the new girls?"

Mr. Havens's weekend worksheet was titled,

"You Have a Second Grade Friend Who—"

Each worksheet had nine boxes in it, and every box included a cute drawing. The drawings had been done by "Mrs. Coach," the girls whispered, Mr. Havens's probably beautiful wife. Each box had a description written in it, such as:

"Who likes to sing!"

"Who has a dog!"

"Who plays basketball!"

Mr. Havens's students were told to write down the name of a classmate who matched that description.

They were supposed to know all the kids in class by now, Alfie guessed.

That was probably the whole point of their weekend homework.

"So what did you do?" EllRay asked. "Just make stuff up—as usual?"

"Be quiet. I do not do that," Alfie said. But she started to giggle.

"Come on," EllRay teased in a coaxing voice. "You can tell me."

"Okay. Maybe I made stuff up, and maybe I didn't," Alfie joked back, keeping her voice low. "I mean, I already know Arletty likes the color red. I know that new girl Bella Babcock has three dogs. And I know Lulu Marino likes fancy clothes. But how am I supposed to know what Scooter Davis and Bryan Martinez like? Not to mention Alan Lewis, who never even talks. I'm not a mind reader."

"You could always ask them," their mother

said, hearing all this as she worked at the kitchen island. "But we need to get going, guys. Dishes in the sink, if you please."

This was telling, not asking.

Mrs. Jakes wrote romantic books for ladies about the olden days. That was how Alfie and EllRay had gotten such weird names. For example, "Alfleta" meant "beautiful elf" in some language from more than a thousand years ago. And "EllRay" was short for "Lancelot Raymond," or "L. Ray."

Lancelot was a handsome knight in a famous old story.

Sometimes her mom got carried away, in Alfie's opinion. Like with baby names.

Because Mrs. Jakes was a writer, she worked at home in Oak Glen, California—unlike her husband, who was a geology professor at a college in San Diego. Dr. Jakes left early for work most weekday mornings.

But even though her mom didn't have to hurry off to a job, there was always a last-minute rush to school, Alfie knew, carrying her bowl and spoon to the sink. This probably happened even on Mars! Alfie could just picture blobby little Martians leaving behind their field trip permission slips and tiny four-armed sweaters as they rushed out the door of their glowing pod-house each morning.

"No offense, Mom," Alfie said, dragging her mind back to planet Earth as she sloshed water in her empty cereal bowl. "But I'm not about to ask some strange boy if he's scared of the dark, or if he loves the color orange. And anyway," she added, taking the lunch and snack bags her mom was handing her, "I didn't have any boys from my class hanging around the house this weekend. *Luckily,*" she added under her breath. "So there was no one to ask."

"But the boys can't be too strange by now," Mrs. Jakes said, not giving up. "And it would be nice to get to know them better, wouldn't it? You used to be friends with lots of little boys when you were in daycare and kindergarten, sweetie," she reminded her daughter.

Alfie and EllRay swapped glances and tried not to laugh. "That was a long time ago, Mom,"

Alfie said. "Second grade is different."

"And Alfie's got her hands full with the *girls* in her class," EllRay chimed in.

"That's not true," Alfie said, frowning. "All the girls are my friends. Basically," she added, hoping it was true.

"Now, maybe," EllRay said, a look of doubt passing across his face.

Alfie's brother sometimes called himself "the voice of experience"—about Oak Glen Primary School, anyway.

The thirteen girls in Alfie's class *had* kind of shape-shifted roughly into groups of three, she admitted to herself. But they were friendly groups of three.

No drama.

During these first four weeks of second grade, everything had been pretty chill, as EllRay would say—and fun.

And all Alfie wanted was for things to stay that way forever.

Freeze!

Just like in the playground game.

In her case, she mostly hung out with Arletty Jackson—her old pal from Kreative Learning and Daycare who had brown skin like herself—and with Phoebe Miller, a new girl in class, with whom she and Arletty had made friends.

Phoebe was nice, and she was funny in a quiet way. She had straight blond hair and blushed—a lot. Seeing Phoebe blush was like watching a chameleon change color.

"Do you have everything?" their mom asked Alfie and EllRay, who almost always got himself to school, usually by bike. But today, he was going somewhere after school with a friend. Mrs. Jakes tossed her car keys up and then snatched them out of the air like a race car driver. "Don't make me drive to school without you," she teased. "Hanni is waiting for us."

Hanni Sobel was Alfie's neighbor-friend, classmate, and carpool buddy. But at school, Hanni hung out mostly with Suzette Monahan and Lulu Marino. That was *her* "group of three" these days.

"I'm ready, Mom. I don't want to be late," Alfie said, her heavy backpack already cradled in her arms. "I want to see if anyone in my class wrote about *me* on their worksheet."

She hoped so, if it was something nice. Or funny.

"They probably did," EllRay assured her as he buckled his seatbelt. "'*Who can be the biggest pain in the neck?*'" he said, pretending to read aloud from a worksheet. "'*Who likes to twirl around and get dizzy until they just about hurl?' 'Who loves to hog all the cheese?*'"

"That's enough, EllRay," Mrs. Jakes said from the front seat as she backed out the driveway.

"Yeah, *EllRay*," Alfie pretend-scolded, smiling. "Enough, enough, enough."

This was going to be such a great week!

A Secret

"We're here," Alfie said.

She and Hanni scrambled out of Mrs. Jakes' car, eager to get in some playtime before the school day started. Kids had to go through the main door to get to the playground and lunch area, so the girls headed up Oak Glen Primary School's wide front steps.

As usual, Principal James was there in his suit and tie, greeting each student by name. "Miss Jakes! And Hanni Sobel, as I live and breathe," he called out, giving them a cheerful wave. He patted the brown mustache Alfie did not like.

She didn't think men's faces should be fancy that way.

“Hi,” the girls mumbled back, waving as best they could, given the sagging backpacks they were lugging up the steps.

“Let’s go,” Hanni urged like a small cheerleader as they charged down the crowded hall.

Both the school and the big playground behind it were divided into two parts. Indoors, the two-story main part of the school held all the classrooms—kindergarten through third grade downstairs, and fourth through sixth grades upstairs. A breezeway near the office led to the cafeteria and auditorium.

Outside, in the back, there was a big asphalt playground with basketball hoops, swings, and structures to climb on. The lunch area on the far side of the playground was scattered with picnic tables and a few trees. This was usually where the girls in Alfie’s class gathered each morning. At one end of the playground, a path sloped down to a play area built only last summer.

One or two giggling girls were already eating their recess snacks early at the picnic table. For a moment, the sound of happy chatter seemed to float above the girls like an invisible rainbow.

"Hey, Pheeb," Alfie said to Phoebe with a smile, flinging her backpack onto the table. "You look cute today. Where's Arletty?"

"Not here yet," Phoebe said, tucking a lock of blond hair behind one pink ear. "Maybe she has the sniffles or something."

"I don't think so," Alfie said, thinking about it. "Probably her mom's just late. Arletty is, like, the healthiest kid I know. That's why she can run so fast."

Alfie and Phoebe both took pride in Arletty's skill, as if their friendship with her had caused Arletty's talent to rub off on them, somehow.

"What are *they* talking about?" Alfie asked in a quiet voice, tilting her head toward Hanni, Suzette, and Lulu, who clustered against the chain-link fence behind the picnic tables. They were whispering. Lulu seemed to be doing most of the talking.

"I don't know," Phoebe said, shrugging.

Hanni's wavy dark hair, Suzette's brown hair, and Lulu's black hair—with the long, perfectly straight bangs that Alfie suspected Mrs. Marino trimmed every morning using a ruler and tiny golden scissors—seemed to blend together into one big tangled head as they talked.

Lulu saw Alfie looking at them, and she shifted her body as if to give their group more privacy.

And Alfie and Lulu used to be best friends just last year, in first grade! A hundred years ago, Alfie thought now.

Somebody had a secret, she knew. And suddenly, this was no longer the perfect September morning she had hoped it would be.

Even though it was warm, Alfie shivered.

The invisible rainbow above the girls' heads had turned into a stormy little cloud.

The newest girl in class sidled up to Alfie and Phoebe like a spy. It was Bella Babcock, the girl with three dogs.

Bella had joined Mr. Havens's class two weeks late. Alfie remembered the exact moment she decided to give her a personal tour of Oak Glen Primary School. Bella was eating her recess snack all alone, as if that were the most important job in the world. Her only job.

No talking, no laughing, no smiling, even.

And Alfie had suddenly thought, *What if that was me? What if* I *was the new kid at a brand-new school?*

"Wanna hang out?" she had asked Bella, who seemed suddenly to melt a little, hearing her words. "I can show you around if you want."

"I guess," Bella had said, shrugging—but smiling, too, as she ducked her head. "I mean, okay. I don't mind."

"Maybe you do, and maybe you don't?" Alfie had teased.

"I *don't* mind," Bella had said, laughing. "Let's go!"

Bella was nice. She had a short, tufty haircut that looked cute on her, a wide smile, and freckles scattered across her nose like a dash of cinnamon.

"I think someone's giving a party," Bella murmured now in an excited, husky voice, glancing over at Hanni, Suzette, and Lulu, who were still whispering. "That girl Lulu, I think it is. A *sleepover*."

She said the last word as if it were a very special thing.

"Great," Phoebe said, breaking into a smile. "Because my cousin goes to sleepovers all the time, and she loves them. It sounds like fun."

"But you told me your cousin's in fifth grade," Alfie reminded Phoebe. "We're only in second grade. Have you even *gone* to a sleepover yet, Pheeb?"

Alfie had, in first grade—though it had been more an overnight babysitting thing than the real deal. And it had not ended well.

First, Alfie had gotten homesick—after only half an hour.

Then her stomach started to hurt.

Then the worst had happened. *Blarrrt!* All over her brand-new pink and purple Fairy Kitties sleeping bag, which was not as washable as the label bragged it was.

"Lulu says it's gonna be the best sleepover ever," Bella reported. "Like the big girls have. And it's this Saturday night! But Lulu's not inviting *everyone.* Only her best friends." She sounded as if she really wanted to go.

"It'll be fun, if it really happens," Phoebe said again. But she sounded a little less sure of herself this time.

"And if we get invited," Alfie pointed out—because Lulu Marino was an up-and-down kind of girl when it came to being, and staying, friends.

"My special darling," her mom called her, Lulu bragged.

"Well, Lulu said she's deciding *this week* who she's gonna ask," Bella said.

"But the rule at Oak Glen Primary School is that you have to ask everyone in class, if you have a party," Phoebe pointed out, the usual blush flooding her cheeks. "Or else you aren't allowed to talk about it at school at all. So Lulu's breaking the rules. She could get in trouble."

"But if we tell on her," Alfie said, "we won't get invited for *sure*."

"Yeah. You're right," Phoebe said, her blue eyes wide with alarm. "And anyway, who would we tell? Mr. Havens?" she asked as the warning buzzer sounded, and most of the girls started gathering their things.

Alfie, Phoebe, and Bella stared at each other for a moment. To the second grade girls' surprise, they all liked their "boy teacher" just fine, they had slowly agreed over the past four weeks. But he hadn't really been tested yet.

Did he "get" girls?

Not to mention important girl-stuff such as sleepovers?

And how would he handle a big deal like this, if someone tattled on Lulu?

"We'd better keep our mouths shut," Alfie said as they hurried across the playground toward the main school building.

"I guess you're right," Phoebe agreed. "Because I want to go to that party, even if Lulu doesn't really know me yet. I'll *make* her know me," she vowed.

Wow! Phoebe was gutsier than she thought, Alfie told herself.

Bella didn't say a word.

But Alfie admitted silently to herself that she wanted to be invited, too.

Even though she didn't know *why* she wanted to go.

Shared Reading

"Listen up, All-Stars," Mr. Havens called out to his students as Alfie was stowing her backpack in the cubby room.

Each class at Oak Glen Primary School had a name, and Alfie's class was called the "All-Stars."

The girls hadn't gotten to vote on it. No one had.

"Bottoms in chairs, people," Mr. Havens—"Coach"—said from his very great height. He used to play basketball in college, EllRay had told Alfie more than once. He was very strong. Even his neck looked strong, Alfie thought. It went straight down from his small, muscle-y ears into his shirt.

"Hup, hup," Mr. Havens said, urging his students to hurry. "We have shared reading and a

writing workshop to get under our trendy little belts before morning recess. So settle down while I take attendance."

"Trendy little belts!" That was probably a jokey dig aimed at Lulu or Suzette, Alfie thought, hiding a smile. Mr. Havens liked to tease them about how fussy they were with their "outfits," as the girls liked to call the clothes they wore each day.

But Mr. Havens was also always quick with a compliment. For example, he had told Dr. and Mrs. Jakes during Back to School Night that Alfie was "as bright as a button." He said it was a pleasure having her in his class, they told her.

A *button*?

"Bright as a button" wasn't as good as cute, talented, adorable, or smart, in Alfie's opinion. But it was better than nothing.

Alfie and Arletty exchanged looks and smiled. Arletty had arrived at school just in time, her mom having got stuck in one of Oak Glen's rare traffic jams.

The All-Stars made their way to the rectangular tables Mr. Havens had placed around the room the first day of school. Five kids sat at each table.

When school first started, Alfie had really wanted to have her own desk and not sit at a group table. A desk seemed more grown-up, more like second grade—or like "the bigs," as Mr. Havens called it, using a sports term, of course.

But now, four weeks in, sharing a table with Arletty, Hanni, Scooter, and a shy new kid named Alan Lewis wasn't so bad after all, she had to admit.

Even though Scooter and Alan were boys.

At the table behind her, Lulu was whispering to Bella—as if she had simply moved her secret conversation inside for a while. "Best sleepover ever," Alfie heard Lulu say to Bella. Bella's eyes were wide.

"Miss Marino," Mr. Havens's voice boomed. "I was not asking a question when I told everyone to settle down. There is no need for any random comments at this time. Save your words for shared reading discussion, please."

The funny thing about shared reading was how good Mr. Havens was at it—reading aloud, and pointing out interesting things in a book, Alfie thought, wriggling her chair closer to the table. He could turn his boomy "Coach" voice into just about anything or anyone. An old lady, a spooky tree, a little kid, a penguin, a monster.

He could even sound like a nature scientist, which was probably the voice he would use today as he read *The Awesome Hummingbird.*

"This will be our shared reading book for the entire week," Mr. Havens told the kids, holding up his copy so everyone could see. "Five whole days. And when we're done, you guys will be All-Star hummingbird experts."

Next to her, Alfie could almost hear Scooter Davis grumbling—without making a sound. *"Yo, who even* wants *to know about hummingbirds?"* he was probably thinking. *"Lame! They're the littlest birds in the world. Girly-birds. Like bugs, almost. Let's hear about vultures! Or pterodactyls."*

Alfie considered herself to be an expert on what—and how—boys thought. She'd had a lot of experience with her big brother EllRay, after all. Living with a brother was like having a student from another country living in the same house, Alfie sometimes thought. She had seen a movie about that once.

"Remember, no Velcro sneaker noises during shared reading," Mr. Havens warned everyone, though he gave Scooter Davis an extra-sharp look. "Or the noisemaker will be asked to perform a little dance for us all."

Behind Alfie, Lulu had continued to whisper through Mr. Havens's instructions. Almost

everyone in class was still a little scared of Mr. Havens at times. But Alfie guessed that Lulu's excitement about her sleepover was bigger than any fear.

Her sleepover was going to be *that good.*

"Miss Marino," Mr. Havens boomed again. He did not sound pleased. "Is there something very urgent that you need to share with everyone in the class? Something important enough to interrupt the learning process of your fellow students? I cannot imagine what that might be. But speak."

"It's not for *everyone,*" Lulu said, sounding more excited than sorry. "Just the girls. For a few of them, I mean. But only a few."

Lulu was talking about the girls she was going to invite to her famous-but-secret sleepover, Alfie thought, sitting up extra straight.

And every single girl in class knew exactly what Lulu was talking about.

"Then we're not interested," Mr. Havens announced.

And he went on to read aloud the first two pages of the hummingbird book.

But she, Alfie Jakes, was *very* interested in what Lulu Marino had to say! In fact, Alfie was barely able to pay attention to the awesomeness of the "little jeweled wonders," as the book called the hummingbirds on the very first page.

Who was Lulu going to invite to her sleepover?

And why was it going to be the "best sleepover ever?"

And what could she do to make sure she got invited?

Finally, what was she going to wear?

She and her mom were going to have to go amazing-jammie shopping, and *soon*.

Like a Wasp at a Picnic Table

"I'm glad you didn't get in trouble for being late to school," Alfie said to Arletty. They were in the cubby room digging in their backpacks for their lunches.

Oak Glen Primary School had a cafeteria, but Mr. Havens's second graders liked to eat outdoors when the weather was nice. And it was perfect today, so that's where most of the kids were headed. Phoebe was already outside, in fact. She was saving places for Alfie and Arletty at the second grade girls' picnic table they liked best.

"Yeah," Arletty said, keeping her voice low as she looked around. "I got here just in time. But what if I had started crying if Mr. Havens yelled at me for being late? *'Crybaby, crybaby, pants on fire,'*" she chanted, copying the pretend kids who might tease her if that ever happened.

"I think it's supposed to be *liars* whose pants are on fire," Alfie said, frowning because even that seemed wrong, didn't it? No matter how much you wished it might be true? Unless it was you doing the fibbing, of course.

"And it's not like I can boss my mom around when she's driving me to school," Arletty said as if Alfie hadn't spoken. Arletty emerged from a crouch, holding her lunch high in the air. Victory!

It was true, Alfie thought, picturing Mrs. Jackson. Arletty's mother was not the kind of mom to put up with any nonsense. Mrs. Jackson was "the human dynamo at every meeting," Alfie's mother had said more than once.

That meant Mrs. Jackson had a lot of energy, she explained to Alfie.

But Mrs. Jackson was nice, and she made very good brownies.

"Come on, Alfie," Arletty said, laughing. "We're missing out on all the fun."

Yeah, fun, Alfie thought with a pang as she

remembered Lulu, and Saturday night's sleepover. How could something so cool—for the invited girls, anyway—make her, Alfie, feel so worried and bad?

Thanks a lot, Lulu!

❋ ❋ ❋

Each outdoors lunch table at Oak Glen was set on a concrete pad surrounded by the world's most worn-out grass. The picnic tables—backed by a chain-link fence—were equal distances apart. They were placed in a line that stretched across the far end of the big playground.

But it was funny how every table seemed different, Alfie thought, looking at them now. Phoebe waved at Alfie and Arletty, her blond hair shining in the sunlight. She pointed down at the two spots she had saved.

This second-grade girls' table was perfect. It was shadier than the others, with little trees planted nearby. Each tree was tied to two tall stakes—which was kind of harsh, Alfie sometimes thought, pitying them.

Alfie and Arletty ran up the small hill to their table, where several girls were talking and eating

lunch. Lulu Marino was the center of attention today, of course. The girls around her were on their best behavior, as if hoping to impress her.

"The point *is*," Lulu was saying, "my sleepover will be just like the ones the big girls have." Hanni nodded and offered her a cookie from a small plastic bag. "So we won't be kindergarten babies anymore," Lulu said, continuing her explanation. "And Mama says I can invite six girls, including me."

Including *her*? Alfie almost burst out laughing. How funny would that be, she wondered—to have a sleepover and not invite yourself?

The only thing weirder would be to *invite* yourself. *"Ooh, thanks! I'd* love *to come to my own party."*

"That means you can ask five girls," Bella said, doing the mental math.

And Lulu was already good friends with Hanni and Suzette, Alfie thought, subtracting with her fingers under the table. So Lulu would only be inviting three other girls to the best sleepover ever.

Including Bella, there was now a total of thirteen girls in their class. And if you subtracted Lulu, Hanni, and Suzette from those thirteen girls, only three out of the ten girls left would be asked to Lulu's sleepover.

And seven girls would not be invited.

This was the only kind of arithmetic that really counted in primary school, Alfie thought, frowning.

"Want me to throw away your trash, Lulu?" Suzette was asking.

"Let me do it for her," Arletty said, jumping to her feet so fast that the shiny red beads at the end of her braids clicked together. And Arletty probably didn't even want to go to the sleepover! She usually did church stuff with her family on the weekends, Alfie knew. She sighed, longing for the good old days—like last week, before Lulu ruined everything with her "just like the big girls" sleepover plans.

Today, though, Lulu was like a wasp at a picnic table. In other words, she was all anyone could think about.

And not in a good way.

Alfie sneaked a peek over at the boys' table and the playground. She actually felt jealous of the fun they were having.

For example, Scooter Davis had drawn a big fancy watch on his wrist during writing workshop. He was pretending to time his friends with it as they took turns sprinting to the nearest battered tree.

Two other boys in her class were having an arm-wrestling contest, their elbows planted on the sticky picnic table. The boys' faces were sweaty, they were grunting, and their arms shook as each boy tried to force the other's arm down, down, down to the tabletop.

But "the point *was*," as Lulu would say, it seemed to be the boys who were having all the fun.

Every single one of them, it looked like.

Did that make Alfie wish she were a boy?

"*No*," she said, way too loud.

She just wished she didn't have to worry so much. This was only the fourth week of school!

"That's weird," Lulu announced to the girls who were still sitting at the table. "Alfie's arguing with herself, it sounds like."

Arletty and Phoebe each shot Alfie a questioning look.

"I'm not arguing with myself," Alfie told everyone. "I was just trying to shoo that wasp away. It had its stinger out and everything," she added, pants on fire.

"What wasp?" a couple of girls said, jumping to their feet in alarm.

"I guess it left," Alfie said. She shrugged modestly and collected her trash.

"Thanks," Lulu said, relieved. "Mama says I should never get stung."

"Because you're allergic?" Suzette asked, eager to be sorry for her in advance.

"Nope. Because it would hurt me," Lulu said.

As if Lulu were *really* such a "special darling," as Mrs. Marino put it, Alfie thought, almost shaking her head in amazement. It would hurt anyone if they got stung by a wasp!

"Thanks, Alfie," Lulu said again as the end-of-lunch warning bell rang. "I really mean it."

"You're welcome," Alfie said, softening a little.

And to her surprise, hope fluttered in her chest.

Maybe she had a chance!

Pretty Little Princess

"Thanks, Mrs. Sobel," Alfie said to Hanni's mom after school the next afternoon, Tuesday. Mrs. Sobel worked at home like Alfie's mother did, so the carpool schedule was perfect most weeks.

Mrs. Sobel gave Alfie a wide smile, and the woman's dangly earrings swayed beneath the perfect straight line of her hair. She was a very tidy lady.

"*Th-h-h-t,*" Alfie and Hanni blurted out to each other in farewell, pushing their tongues through the holes where missing front teeth used to be.

"*Ew,*" they said at the same time.

"Bye, Hanni," Alfie added, still giggling as she slammed shut the car door.

She'd been feeling kind of shy around Hanni for the past day and a half. That was probably because Hanni had become such good friends with Lulu Marino once second grade started. Hanni was, after all, part of Lulu's group of three.

But the carpool face-making and laughter had helped get things back to normal—*for now,* Alfie thought, sighing.

Since Mrs. Sobel and Mrs. Jakes always waited until each girl was inside her house before driving away, Alfie hurried up the driveway to her kitchen door instead of dawdling. And dawdling—goofing around doing nothing—was one of her favorite things to do.

Alfie eased herself into the kitchen carefully, so Princess wouldn't escape, not that the Jakes' small gray kitten seemed at all interested in getting out.

Princess was a late-summer gift from the Sobels. Alfie and EllRay thought Princess was probably the cutest kitten in the world. Almost thirteen weeks old now, Princess had eyes that had turned from blue to a golden-green, and her ears looked two sizes too big for her silky head.

"Clown-kitty," EllRay sometimes called her now, teasing.

"Princess!" Alfie called out in the empty kitchen. "Mom, I'm home!"

Where was her welcoming committee?

Her mother's car was in the driveway, Alfie knew, so she was probably finishing a chapter in the new book she was writing. And Princess was most likely asleep.

Taking naps seemed to be their kitten's favorite hobby.

But she, Alfie, was *starving.* Alfie heaved her backpack onto the kitchen island and headed for the fridge.

"Peanut butter and jelly sandwich. Peanut butter and jelly sandwich," she recited to herself. "And an icy-cold glass of milk," she added, her stomach gurgling.

Out of nowhere, just as Alfie sat down at the kitchen table with her after-school snack, Princess came skidding into the kitchen—as if she had only now learned that Alfie was home. The kitten clawed her way up Alfie's leggings like she was climbing a tree. "Ouch," Alfie said, plucking Princess off her leg. She cuddled her close for a moment.

Princess started purring, her kitty motor turned up high.

Purr. Purr-r. Purr-r-r.

"Pretty little Princess," Alfie said through a mouthful of smooth peanut butter and grape jelly as she munched her way through her first bite of sandwich. Then she hugged her kitty as tight as Princess would allow. Alfie could feel her own heart fill up with something warm and sweet, like hot chocolate with a gooey marshmallow on top.

That's how good having a kitty made Alfie feel—as if she could tell Princess *anything,* and the kitten would get it.

"You probably already know this, Princess," Alfie began, "but I don't even really *like* sleepovers. Not since I hurled all over my Fairy Kitties sleeping bag that time. Mom finally had to throw it away, because it wouldn't wash right," she told her kitty. "Even though that sleepover was really more of a babysitting night, not a party," she added, correcting herself. "But I got homesick almost right away," she confessed into Princess's soft, gray fur.

Purr. Purr-r. Purr-r-r-r.

Princess loved her no matter what, Alfie thought, relieved.

"So why do I even want to *go* to Lulu's goofy sleepover?" she asked aloud. "Two reasons," she said, as if Princess was waiting for the answer. "First, I want to see why Lulu says this will be 'the best sleepover ever,'" she told her kitten. "I mean, how good can a sleepover be? And *why* is it going to be so great? Is she ordering pizzas for everyone? Or handing out really cool party favors?" she asked.

Purr. Purr-r. Purr-r-r-r-r.

"Or maybe there are gonna be some super-fun games," Alfie said, working her way through her sandwich. "And prizes. Or there might be ghost stories right before going to bed," she added, shivering with pleasure. "Who knows?"

Princess gazed up at Alfie—like she was asking her a question.

"Okay, okay," Alfie said, as if confessing a secret. "All that stuff is only *kinda* true. Because the

main thing is, *I don't want not to be invited.* That's all. I mean, if we're going to be 'just like the big girls,' I want in," she added, trying to make things clearer. "Or else I'll be *o-u-t.* And who wants to be left out? Not me."

Purr. Purr-r. Purr-r-r-r-r-r.

Her kitty agreed with her, Alfie thought, giving Princess a hug that was only a little bit sticky.

Princess understood.

Absolutely.

Great Advice

"Knock, knock," Alfie said after dinner, rapping on EllRay's bedroom door.

"Come in, I *guess*," EllRay called out. "Only you don't have to knock on my door *and* say 'knock, knock,' Alf," he added. He was stretched out on his bed, doing his homework. "One of 'em is enough. Two of 'em is one too many."

"Huh?" Alfie said, peeking around the door.

Her brother was long, skinny, and strong, and Alfie was secretly proud of him. It was like she got extra points at school for having a brother in sixth grade.

"Never mind," EllRay said, laughing.

"Are you busy?" Alfie asked. She sat down in

EllRay's desk chair, which he almost never used.

"Just hangin' with a bunch of possessive pronouns," EllRay said. "Why? Are you having trouble with your dreaded fraction circles homework?"

Alfie had been complaining about it during dinner. At Oak Glen Primary School, the kids were supposed to get ten minutes of homework for each grade they were in. So being in second grade meant twenty minutes of homework a night, not counting reading. Sixth graders had sixty minutes of homework—only it usually ended up being a lot more, according to EllRay.

"The math part of the homework was easy," Alfie said, picturing the circles on her worksheet. They were divided into two parts, or three parts, or four, five, or six parts each. She was supposed to look at the fraction written next to each circle—$^{1}/_{2}$, $^{2}/_{3}$, $^{3}/_{5}$, $^{2}/_{5}$—and color in that many parts of the circle.

"But math is the whole thing," EllRay pointed out. "That's why they call it 'math homework.' So what's the problem?"

"Keeping my colored pencils sharp enough so the little pieces of pie look colored-in just perfect," Alfie told him.

"That's not an important part of the homework," EllRay said, laughing.

"It is for us girls," Alfie said, giving him a look. "It'll be like a contest, almost. You should see how good Lulu and Suzette are at shading stuff in. They could do it for a living, they're so great. They never scribble-scrabble at all."

"Suzette Monahan?" EllRay asked, frowning. "Is she still around?"

Alfie and Suzette had been on-again, off-again friends since preschool, when Suzette had become famous in the Jakes family for demanding a trip to McDonald's during her first playdate with Alfie. In fact, Alfie's dad still called any attempt at bossy kid behavior "pulling a Suzette."

"She's my friend, for better or worse," Alfie said, slumping in the chair. "*All* the girls in my class are my friends, I already told you."

"Okay, okay," EllRay said, holding up his hands in pretend surrender. "I give. And I totally believe you. So what's the problem? Or did you just wanna talk? Because—"

He rattled a few of the papers surrounding him.

"I get it," Alfie grumbled. "You have lots of homework because you're an important sixth grader who's the boss of the world."

"The boss of Oak Glen Primary School, maybe," EllRay said, pretending to think about it. "What's up?" he asked again.

"It's Tuesday, right?" Alfie said. "And everything was going perfect with the girls in my class until yesterday morning. That's when Lulu Marino said she's gonna have a sleepover this Saturday night. The best sleepover ever, in fact. But her mom says she can only invite five other girls, and she has to decide this week who they're gonna be. And two girls are already her best friends. Suzette and Hanni."

"So that leaves three empty spaces," EllRay said, doing the math. "But you should get in easy, right? Because you and Lulu are so tight."

"Yeah, sure," Alfie said, making a face. "*Last*

year, maybe. I mean, we didn't have a fight or anything," she hurried to explain. "Things just kinda changed over the summer when she went to Maine. I don't know why. But I still want to go to the sleepover. I just don't know how to pull it off."

EllRay twiddled his pencil so fast while he thought that it became a yellow blur. "Wait," he said, his eyes narrowing, and the pencil blur

stopped. "Lulu's not supposed to be talking about parties at school, is she? Not unless she invites every single girl in your class. So she's breaking the rules. You should tell her she has to invite all the girls. That's what."

"She probably wouldn't listen, *that's what,*" Alfie said, shaking her head. "And nobody's going to say anything to Mr. Havens about it, either," she added. "Or Lulu won't invite them *for sure.* Besides, Mr. Havens is just a boy, basically," Alfie said. "And that means he could never understand us girls in a million years. And this is exactly what I was worried about way back last summer, remember? Having a boy teacher? I was right!"

"That was only four weeks ago," EllRay pointed out. "And how do you think us boys feel? I've had a so-called 'girl teacher' every single year so far at Oak Glen."

"But girl teachers understand *everybody,*" Alfie told him.

"No, they don't," EllRay said, snapping out the words. "You could ask Mom what to do, but parents get all mad at each other when their kids' feelings get hurt. It just ends up making everything worse."

"Yeah," Alfie said.

"What about if you remind Lulu you used to be best friends?" EllRay asked.

"That's too lame," Alfie said.

"Then do something nice for her," EllRay suggested.

"But everyone's already kissing up to Lulu," Alfie argued. "She's as happy as a piggy in a puddle. You should see her."

"Then give her a present so she'll invite you," EllRay said, only half paying attention now.

"That's your great advice?" Alfie asked. "What am I supposted to give her, a bag full of money? Real money?"

"Unless you can get her to take Monopoly money," EllRay said, laughing.

"That's lame, too," Alfie scoffed. "Either kind of money. Anyway," she added, thinking about it. "I'm not gonna pay somebody to be my friend."

"I was kidding," EllRay said. "Even if you did

want to pay her, you're broke. And *I'm* not lending you anything."

"Who cares?" Alfie said. "But I'm not getting any closer to going to Lulu's sleepover, am I?" she asked, scowling.

Alfie could feel hot tears gather at the corners of her eyes. Her family called this "clouding up," as if Alfie were a day that could turn from sunny to stormy, just like that.

"Wait a minute," EllRay said, putting his pencil aside. "Maybe I can help. Talk to me, but pretend that you're talking to Lulu, okay? Because maybe she doesn't know how much you wanna go to her party."

"Huh," Alfie said. But she was listening.

"I'll be Lulu, and you be you," EllRay explained.

"Wait," Alfie protested. "How come I have to be me? I always have to be me. I should get to be somebody else, for a change."

"Let's just try it my way first," EllRay said, sighing.

"Okay. But you start," she told her brother.

EllRay groaned, but then he spoke. *"I'm giving*

this totally awesome party on Saturday, yo," he began in a high voice, pretending to be Lulu. *"And it's gonna be pretty chill."*

"But your mom says you can only ask a few girls," Alfie said, coaching him. "Go on, say it, EllRay. Except Lulu Marino's mom calls her a special darling, so she never says 'yo.'"

EllRay gave a dramatic sigh. *"But my mom says I can only ask a few girls,* yo," he said, still in Alfie's face a little as he peeped out the last word.

"Really?" Alfie said in a pretend-casual, too-sweet voice. "Because I just love parties, Lulu! You remember that from when we were best friends last year, right? And I'm not doing anything on Saturday. Especially on Saturday night."

"That's interesting," EllRay-Lulu said.

"Phoebe loves parties too," Alfie said, as if she'd just been thinking about it. "And so does Bella Babcock, the new girl with three dogs. Amazing dogs," she added, exaggerating.

But she didn't know, Alfie told herself. Maybe Bella's dogs *were* amazing.

"Oh! You guys should definitely come," EllRay-Lulu said, pretending to fluff up his invisible hair.

"Lulu would never say it that easy," Alfie argued, becoming her regular self again. "She'd stretch it out and make me beg."

"You're kidding me," EllRay said, frowning. "Then why do you want to go so bad? Who needs her, if she's like that?"

"*I* do," Alfie explained, after thinking about it. "Because she's the one giving the sleepover." *Duh.*

"Pathetic," EllRay said, shaking his head. "You're better than that, Alf. You gotta stand up to her, if she's really acts that way! Or at least stand up for what you want."

"You just don't get it, that's all," Alfie told him, jumping up from her brother's chair. "I don't know why I even bothered asking for advice! *You're* not a girl."

"You just figured that out?" EllRay asked, laughing again.

"I should ask my friends, instead," Alfie told him. "*They'll* help me decide what to do."

"If anything," EllRay said, and he turned back to his pronouns.

"What's that supposed to mean?" Alfie asked, pausing at the door.

"It means that sometimes, you don't do anything," EllRay told her. "You just let things happen the way they happen."

"Huh!" Alfie said-snorted. "That's sure not *my* motto."

"I know that," EllRay said, still smiling as he shook his head. "Bye, Alfie," he told her. "Hint, hint."

"Good-bye *yourself*," Alfie said, eager to have the last word.

Brothers. Hah!

Miffed, Hurt, Irked, and Furious

"Let's go hang out at the campfire," Phoebe said to Alfie at morning recess the next day, Wednesday.

"Okay," Alfie said. "After I go to the restroom. You go ahead. I'll catch up."

Recesses at Oak Glen Primary School were set at different times for different grades, so the hall was not too crowded as Alfie headed toward the girls' room. But as she was about to pull open the restroom's heavy door, out charged Lulu Marino. Lulu looked excited, and her face was pink, as if she had just won a tetherball game on a very hot day.

"Move it," Lulu exclaimed, bumping into Alfie

in the doorway. "And mind your own business, while you're at it."

"Hey," Alfie said. "I *am* minding my own business."

Because what business could be more personal than a visit to the restroom?

"Don't say it that way," Lulu warned. "And the point *is*, you know what I mean."

"Not really," Alfie muttered, making her way into the restroom.

Lulu could be so weird, Alfie told herself, trying to hold her breath for as long as she could. It wasn't that the girls' restroom smelled nasty most of the time, but there was always that possibility. And the too-sweet smell of foamy handwashing liquid mixed with the sharp odor of whatever it was the custodian used to clean the floor at night was gross, in Alfie's opinion.

Today, though, the only unusual thing going on in the girls' room was the sound coming from behind the closed door of one of the restroom stalls.

Some girl was crying, Alfie realized, horrified. Crying! With great gulpy sobs!

Alfie froze. Crying at school was way up there on Alfie's list of nightmares-come-true, right after wetting yourself at school and hurling in class. But there were three kinds of school crying.

There was crying on the playground if you got hurt, which was okay. Not great, but okay—because you'd been wounded in battle, basically.

And then there was crying in front of other kids if you heard something really sad, like a dog dying in a story, or if someone hurt your feelings on the playground. That was embarrassing, but it was understandable.

Crying all alone in the bathroom, though? That was just *sad*.

The only thing worse would be for someone to see you doing it.

But just as Alfie unfroze enough to make a dash for a stall before the crying girl could exit hers, the other girl's tan metal door swung open—and out came Bella, mopping at her splotchy, swollen face with a handful of tissue-y toilet paper squares. "Oh!" she said, seeing Alfie. "I'm sorry. And I'm not really crying."

"Okay. Fine," Alfie mumbled, disappearing into her stall.

Phew! Close one, Alfie thought, latching the door.

And by the time she went to wash her hands, Bella was long gone.

The new play area was sunken, sandy, and shady. It had two slides, "one straight and one curly," the littlest kids in school boasted. There was also a circle of upended logs to sit on. Alfie and her friends had started calling this area "the campfire," even though there was never a fire in the middle, of course.

It was just an ordinary day, Alfie told herself as Phoebe greeted her on the sloping path, and they walked toward the log circle. But the day seemed to have its own sour personality—in spite of that morning's cloudless blue September sky. The only second grade girl who truly seemed happy today, Alfie thought, was Lulu Marino, the "special darling" sleepover queen.

Bella was nowhere to be seen.

"Were you really best friends with Lulu last

year?" Phoebe whispered. She had moved to Oak Glen from Arizona over the summer, and she was still catching up on the other girls' stories.

"I guess," Alfie said again. She tried to remember that far back.

Alfie and Lulu had often played dolls when they were on playdates together. Even then, Lulu liked more to fuss with the dolls' small clothes than to make up stories about them. And making up stories was one of Alfie's favorite things to do.

The two girls used to watch cartoons, too—more at Lulu's house than at Alfie's, because Alfie's parents had so many rules about TV during the day at their house.

The girls even invented a silly but fun game they called "Upside-Down Heads," where they would lie on the grass, their heads together but their bodies stretched out in opposite directions. How funny Lulu had looked then, with her eyes seeming to be at the bottom of her face, perched atop her straight bangs! And she herself must have looked unfamiliar too, Alfie guessed, with her mouth where her eyes were supposed to be.

They even tried drawing pictures of each other that way.

It was hard to remember exactly *why* this had been such a crack-up when they were six years old, Alfie thought now. But she and Lulu had giggled a lot. That much she remembered.

And then Lulu went to Maine with her family all last summer, a summer that had felt to Alfie as though it lasted an entire year.

But even before that, she and Lulu had stopped hanging out as much as before, Alfie had to admit.

Things changed, her mom often remarked.

"Look at them," Phoebe whispered as they approached the circle of logs. "Nobody looks very happy, except for Lulu and Suzette."

It was true, Alfie saw. Instead of laughing, or even smiling, the girls looked miffed, hurt, irked, and, in Hanni Sobel's case, furious.

And Hanni was one of Lulu's two best friends at school this year!

"Maybe this means Hanni's not getting invited to the sleepover," Phoebe whispered, sounding excited—as if she was happy that another vacancy might have opened up on Lulu's guest list.

"That's messed-up, Pheeb," Alfie said, surprised. Phoebe was usually so sweet!

Were her second grade classmates really going to turn on each other now?

Alfie walked over to where Hanni was sulking on a log. She whispered, "Are you okay, Hanni? What's the matter?"

"I don't know," Hanni mumbled, her green eyes narrowing as she looked away.

She didn't know! And Hanni Sobel, "the world's oldest seven-year-old," according to Alfie's mom, was kind of a know-it-all, Alfie had to admit. Even EllRay said so. It was rare for Hanni to say "I don't know" about *anything.*

"Only I'm not giving Lulu my dessert at lunch, no matter what she says," Hanni blurted out. "My mom made chocolate chip cookies last night, and I'm eating mine."

Well, *that* group of three was gonna change, Alfie thought, surprised.

"Listen to me!" Lulu's voice suddenly soared over all the other log circle sounds: over the chittering of cranky squirrels, and over the squawks of blue and gray California scrub jays who were yelling at each other like kindergarteners.

Over the laughter of little kids on both the straight and curly slides.

Over the angry whispers of second grade girls perched on logs.

Suzette, now *unhappy,* glared at Phoebe with suspicion.

Hanni was kicking at the log she sat on with the heel of her shoe.

Even Arletty—who would probably be busy doing church stuff with her family the night of the sleepover—had folded her arms across her chest as if someone was about to give her a shove. She looked really upset.

Huh, Alfie thought, starting to get mad. Lulu was ruining everything!

"Listen to me," Lulu said again to the gloomy assortment of second grade girls. "I'm not saying yes to *anybody* yet about the sleepover, and I'm not saying no, either. Except to that new girl, Bella. I'm saying that I'm still deciding, that's all. And I have two more days to make up my mind," she added. "I'll tell you for sure who's coming on Friday afternoon. But until then, I'm—"

"Stop it," Alfie said, surprising even herself.

She glanced behind her to see who had just spoken.

"What?" Lulu said, snapping her head around so fast that her perfect straight bangs swayed like a short, dark curtain above her angry eyes. "*What* did you just say to me, Alfie Jakes?"

"I said stop it," Alfie told her. Her heart thudded as the other girls began melting away from the log circle, eager to escape. They would be heading back to class early, for once. "I have to talk to you now, Lulu," Alfie added. "In private," she added to show how serious she was.

Lulu looked at her wrist as if checking the time.

"You're not wearing a watch," Alfie said. "And we have time. It's important," she added, trying for a smile. "Come on, Upside-Down Head," she added, hoping Lulu would remember their silly old game.

"*Hmmph,*" Lulu snorted. "I *guess* I have time. So, okay."

"Okay, then," Alfie echoed, waiting for the last straggler to leave.

Uh-Oh

"So, what do you want?" Lulu asked Alfie after an awkward moment or two. "You know the buzzer is about to go off. I have a perfect record so far for being prompt, and I am not gonna let you mess that up."

Alfie had a perfect record, too, or almost. But she didn't waste time pointing that out. She was trying to think of what to say. And then inspiration struck. "I think you should invite every girl in our class to your sleepover, that's what," she said, stealing EllRay's idea from the the night before. "Because everything was so perfect for the first four weeks of school, Lulu! But ever since Monday, things have been terrible around here. And *you made Bella cry*," she added.

"Liar," Lulu snapped. "You'd better not tell anyone about that, either. And things haven't been terrible for *me*," she added, thinking about it. "Also, I know five other girls who will be happy on Friday when they get their invitations. By the way, *Alfie*, you were gonna be one of them," she said, shaking her head in pity. "But too bad, because you just made me look dumb in front of everyone."

Lulu was doing that all by herself, Alfie thought, pressing her lips together so that more words wouldn't spill out and make things worse.

Because—uh-oh! Lulu was really mad at her.

"I only said I wanted to talk to you," Alfie tried to explain. "Why did that make you look dumb?"

"Anyway," Lulu said, ignoring the question, "I already told you. Mama said I could invite five other girls. Not eleven or twelve. That's almost twice as many as five."

Okay, Alfie thought—she wasn't gonna touch that arithmetic mistake. "But I'm sure some girls wouldn't be able to come," she told Lulu, trying to back up her suggestion. "And everyone could bring her own sleeping bag and sleep on the floor. You could squeeze them all in, Lulu! Your house is huge. They could bring their own food, too, so your mom wouldn't have to—"

"It's not 'everyone's' sleepover, Alfie," Lulu interrupted in a pretend-patient voice. "It's *mine.* And Mama made the rules about how many girls I could invite."

Oof. Lulu was making some pretty good points, Alfie admitted to herself.

Bad idea, EllRay! This was all his fault, Alfie told herself, scowling.

"And you can't tell other people how to throw a party," Lulu continued. "Or who to invite, no matter how wonderful and cute you think you are. You're not so great, Alfie Jakes."

"I absolutely do not think I'm so great," Alfie objected, her heart thudding. "But if you're talking about *rules,* you forgot a big one, Lulu. At our school, you're not supposed to tell kids about parties if you're not inviting everyone."

"Oh. So now I have to invite the boys, too?" Lulu scoffed, as if that's what Alfie was saying. "You want me to ask *twenty-six kids* to my sleepover? That's just silly!"

"That's not what I meant," Alfie told her.

"You are *definitely* not coming to the best sleepover ever on Saturday, Alfie," Lulu said, getting to her feet. "But I guess this means that now you're going to tell on me for just barely mentioning the sleepover at school? And for supposedly making Bella cry?"

By now, Alfie was so mad that she felt like her way-too-hot head was about to pop. "I never said I was gonna tell on you," she said, trying to sound calm.

"It's not my fault if I'm the fun one around here," Lulu said, straightening her outfit before stalking up the slope so she could hurry to class.

"But what happened to us being friends?" Alfie called after her, trying to catch up. "Don't you even remember, Lulu? Our dolls? The cartoons?"

"I could never be friends with a tattletale!" Lulu shouted over her shoulder.

And just like that, Alfie thought, *she* was the bad guy.

Huh?

As they entered the nearly empty main hall, Alfie tried to imagine using her own strong fingers to turn back the metal hands of the big, tick-y clock that hung above the school office. If she could turn back time, she could change her mind about talking to Lulu.

Would she?

Maybe I would, and maybe I wouldn't, Alfie admitted to herself.

She honestly didn't know for sure.

"You were trying to boss my mama around, that's what you were doing," Lulu said, lowering her voice as they hurried down the echoing hall toward class. "And I'm telling *everyone.*"

"Telling them what?" Alfie whisper-shouted. "That I wanted to keep you from hurting other girls' feelings?"

"Not *everyone*'s feelings," Lulu argued again, pausing at Mr. Havens's closed classroom door. "And I *am* telling the other girls about how you tried to ruin my sleepover."

"And then who's gonna be the tattletale around here?" Alfie cried just as Mr. Havens opened the door.

"Ladies?" he said, looming over them.

He sounded calm—but scary.

"Meet Your Neighbors!"

"Ooh! Trouble," Bryan Martinez said with glee as Mr. Havens marched the two girls to their tables. Scooter high-fived his hand in the air across the room toward Bryan.

Scooter sat right next to Alfie, so she saw the whole thing.

And she *liked* Bryan. He was okay, usually.

"No more noise from you, Mr. Martinez," Mr. Havens said as he waited for Alfie to take her seat. Then he led Lulu to the table behind Alfie's.

"Okay, Coach," Bryan said, cheerful in spite of the scolding.

"We didn't mean to be late, Mr. Havens," Alfie told her teacher, deciding to take the blame. "But I had to talk to Lulu about something really important. *Personal* and important. So it was my fault we—"

"Social Studies is important too," Mr. Havens interrupted. "And so is my time."

"Is this going on my permanent record?" Lulu asked as Mr. Havens sat her down. "Because Alfie's not even my friend anymore."

A *zing!* of excitement went through every girl in class.

Especially Alfie.

"I'll decide later about your permanent record," Mr. Havens said. "Bella?" he asked. "Give Alfie and Lulu their 'Meet Your Neighbors!' worksheets, please. They can catch up with the rest of us the best they can."

Bella had been standing near Mr. Havens's desk, a few drooping papers in her hand. Her nose was still pink from crying in the bathroom. Bella handed Alfie what looked like a map of the United States and whispered, "Sorry."

"That's okay," Alfie murmured back, examining the piece of paper.

She didn't know all the states yet. Was she *supposed* to know them?

And—"Meet Your Neighbors!" What did *that* mean?

A week ago, her class had done a worksheet called "I'm on the Map!" that was about their local streets and the town of Oak Glen. Not about all the states in the country.

Mr. Havens was thinking big this week.

"Now, Alan," he said to the new boy at Alfie's table. "Before we were interrupted, we were learning where California is on the map. So, what states are our neighbors? That is, what states touch the California border?"

Alan's face turned pale. He did not like being called on in class.

"I know you know one of the states, Phoebe," Mr. Havens said, switching victims. "You used to live there," he added, giving her a hint.

"Arizona," Phoebe said, beaming.

"And how many North American neighbors does California have other than Arizona?" Mr. Havens asked. "Think fast," he added, making an impatient circle-movement with his gigantic hand.

"Not counting the Pacific Ocean?" Scooter asked when Mr. Havens called on him.

"That's right," Mr. Havens said. "*State* neighbors. *Hup, hup,* All-Stars."

"Two," Hanni said when Mr. Havens called on her. "Nevada and Oregon."

"Correct," Mr. Havens said with a brisk nod. But he was smiling.

❋ ❋ ❋

On and on the Social Studies lesson went, with Mr. Havens hopping all over the map as he asked his questions.

What states had the kids visited?

What states did they *want* to visit?

What states had he and Mrs. Havens visited?

In what states did the kids' grandparents live?

And, always, what were all those states' neighbors?

But Alfie had trouble paying attention. *Has Mr. Havens forgotten that Lulu and I came in late?* she kept asking herself, hoping it was true. *Maybe our trouble is all in the past! And maybe Lulu will forgive me. Maybe both our permanent records are still perfect,* she added silently, crossing her fingers under the table for luck.

Lulu Marino might even change her mind about them not being friends anymore—and invite her to the sleepover!

Arletty leaned over and gave Alfie's shoulder a gentle poke.

"Listen up, Miss Jakes," Mr. Havens was saying again, his unblinking eyes fixed on Alfie's.

"It's almost time for lunch, but I want you to stay behind and help me out with a little something."

Oh no, Alfie thought, alarmed. He was going to yell at her! And everyone knew it.

"You're not gonna be out on the basketball court today, Coach?" Bryan almost wailed. "But you said we would work on our layups! You said!"

"Thanks a lot, *Alfie*," Scooter whispered, giving her the stink-eye.

"Sometimes plans change," Mr. Havens told them, squelching all further comments with a single look from his great height.

Alfie gulped, but she tried to catch her breath at the same time, leading to some major coughing.

Could a girl choke on nothing in class? Would Mr. Havens have to call 9-1-1?

She gripped her "Meet Your Neighbors!" worksheet as if it were the life raft that might save her. But it didn't.

"Stay behind," Mr. Havens said again.

A Pickle

"Don't worry, I won't keep you long," Mr. Havens began, perching on the edge of Alfie's table.

It was like Mr. Havens was a giant in a fairy-tale, Alfie thought, her heart pounding, and she was a tiny villager. She tried to sit up straighter, make herself taller.

"You gotta look him right in the eye," she could almost hear EllRay saying.

"So, I want to you tell me, Alfie," Mr. Havens said. "What's going on around here? With the All-Star girls, I mean. I'm counting on you to communicate with me."

Huh? "But why?" Alfie asked. "I don't know anything."

"You are one of the leaders in class," Mr. Havens said, as if pointing out something obvious.

"How come you think that?" Alfie asked, amazed. "Nobody listens to me—ever!"

"Of course they do," Mr. Havens said, laughing. "Alfie, you talk to other girls when something important comes up, don't you? As it did this morning, it seems. And what about the time you got the kids to help pick up trash on the playground that windy day? I saw that. And didn't you go to the trouble of showing Bella Babcock around school when she enrolled late? She was feeling shy back then."

"I guess," Alfie admitted. "But I was just—"

"You were just being a leader," Mr. Havens said, finishing her sentence.

"But I'm not really the boss of the girls," Alfie pointed out after a long, silent moment. "Hanni's more of the leader-type, Mr. Havens. *Really.* Or Suzette or Lulu, if you're talking about girls who like to tell other kids what to do."

"Leaders aren't always bossy," Mr. Havens said, smiling. "And I think you're more of a leader than you realize, Alfie. You are like a bridge between the old Oak Glen girls, who tend to stick together, and all the other girls—the new ones, the shy ones."

She *was*?

And was that supposed to be a compliment, being called a bridge? Although the Golden Gate Bridge was pretty cool. Alfie's family had visited San Francisco just last summer. She wanted to live there when she grew up.

"Um, thanks, I *guess*," Alfie said, trying to keep her legs from running out of the room—along with the rest of her, of course.

"You're welcome," Mr. Havens said.

"I can't tell you our private business, though," Alfie said before she could chicken out. "It's nothing dangerous, but it's girl stuff. So that would be like tattling on myself *and* my friends."

"I don't mean tattling on anyone," Mr. Havens said, holding up one big hand like a stop sign. "I'm not asking that. But look, I know something has been going on with you girls for the past couple of days. I can't quite tune it in, but I can sense that trouble is brewing. And it concerns me."

He was right, Alfie thought. But if she blabbed

now, she told herself, nothing good would come of it. She would *never* get invited to the sleepover.

She imagined herself friendless and alone before school.

And during morning recess.

At lunch.

And all through afternoon recess.

And after school.

During all the really *important* times of a school day.

It was such a very sad thought that Alfie almost started to cry, pitying her poor, lonely, imaginary self.

She sometimes got carried away like that, her mom claimed.

"Look, Alfie," Mr. Havens said again. "I didn't mean to put you in such a difficult spot. I just want to know about any special concerns or problems you girls might be having, and I thought of asking you. I'm the teacher. Maybe I can help."

That sounded "reasonable," as Alfie's dad might put it. But how could she tell Mr. Havens about the problems the girls were having without saying something about the sleepover? And how could she tell Mr. Havens about Lulu's sleepover without letting him know that Lulu had already broken a school rule?

It was "a pickle," as her mom would say.

And talking to Mr. Havens was only going to make things worse. For *her,* at least.

In a way, Alfie realized suddenly, that was why she wasn't going to be able to ask her friends for advice, either—despite what she had told her brother last night. She couldn't! Because if her friends helped *Alfie* get invited to Lulu's sleepover, it would probably mean they had just crossed themselves off the guest list.

Asking a person—herself included—to goof themself up like that was never a very "reasonable" request.

"I want *all* my All-Stars to be happy," Mr. Havens was saying, "and to have an excellent second grade experience."

"Me too," Alfie said. And she remembered that only two days ago, all she had wanted in the world was for the girls in her class to keep on having fun and to stay friends.

Freeze!

Those were the good old days—before Lulu's sleepover ruined everything.

"Just think about what I said, that's all," Mr. Havens said, standing up. "Because right now, half of my class is pretty unhappy, Miss Jakes. And that makes *me* unhappy."

"Okay," Alfie said, not looking at her teacher. "I'll think about what you said."

But—maybe she would, and maybe she wouldn't, Alfie told herself, trying not to frown.

Wasn't her life complicated enough without having to worry about *him*?

The Yips

"Watch out, everyone," EllRay said as the Jakes family sat down for dinner that night. "Alfie's got the yips. We should put some of those orange traffic cones around her so nobody gets hurt."

"I don't have the yips," Alfie said, trying to kick him under the table.

In the Jakes family, "the yips" meant that someone was really, really nervous. It was one of several expressions they used with each other to describe different moods.

One of the Jakes might have "the sads" for some reason, for example.

Or "the mads."

Or they might be "happy as a bean," when things were going great.

And Alfie *did* have the yips, she admitted silently. But anyone would, if they were in the same pickle that she was in.

She had definitely decided not to talk to any of the girls in her class about the sleepover guest list—or about Mr. Havens's talk with her that afternoon. It was as if there were little cartoon skulls-and-crossbones warning signs around the very idea.

At the dinner table, Alfie's father raised an eyebrow. This was his silent way of asking a question.

Dr. Warren Jakes was tall, thin, and sometimes absent-minded. That was because he was a geology professor, Alfie guessed. He was a real brain. And that brain was often busy thinking about all the things that made up the planet Earth. Especially rocks.

That kind of thinking took time.

But tonight, Alfie had their father's full attention. "Why do you have the yips?" he asked, instantly concerned. "What's up, Alfie? Trouble at school?"

Alfie and EllRay's parents took their children's

education very seriously. They were always on the alert for problems at school.

In fact, Alfie sometimes pictured her father as being a skinny stick-bug with super-long antennae always waving in the air, trying to sense danger.

"Not trouble *at* school," Alfie said, fibbing a little as she crossed her fingers under the table.

Mrs. Jakes was busy serving up helpings of tuna casserole—with melted cheese and buttery breadcrumbs on top, making it edible to Alfie. But she paused, giving her daughter a searching look.

She wasn't exactly lying to her mom and dad, Alfie told herself—because the problem was happening *outside,* on the playground. Not in class. So—

"Alfie?" her father was saying. "Cricket?"

"It's nothing," Alfie mumbled. "Everything's okay. I don't wanna talk about it." She started nibbling at the cheese and breadcrumbs on top of her helping of tuna casserole.

"Those are three entirely different answers," her father pointed out, both eyebrows rising to the middle of his forehead this time.

"Eat the whole serving, sweetie, not just the topping," Alfie's mom told her. "And eat some of those peas, too. You and I will have a private conversation after dinner about those pesky yips. You don't mind if I handle this, do you, Warren?" she asked her husband.

"Not in the least," Alfie's dad said. He sounded relieved.

"Do we have to?" Alfie asked her mom, not looking up from her plate.

"We have to," her mom said, in a way that let Alfie know there was no getting out of it. But Mrs. Jakes sounded calm, too—as though nothing Alfie said could ever upset her.

And for some reason, that made Alfie feel a whole lot better about *everything.*

In a State

"Okay, young lady. Speak to me," Alfie's mom said that night after Alfie had showered and tucked herself into bed. "Everything seemed fine on Monday morning. But now it's Wednesday night, and you're in a state."

"Yeah. California," Alfie said, trying to laugh.

She wriggled further under her covers and pulled them up to her chin. Princess cuddled next to her and started pushing her small paws back and forth against the blanket, as if she were softening it up.

"No. I mean that you're in a bad state of mind, sweetie," her mom explained. "I'm talking about your *mood*. What happened? Are you having trouble with your schoolwork? Problems with your word list?"

"Nuh-uh," Alfie said, shaking her head. Her bedside light was on, and her mom's face looked golden in the light.

Princess continued to purr.

She might as well tell the truth, Alfie thought with a sigh. Her mom wasn't going anywhere, not until she knew what was going on in Mr. Havens's class—or outside, on the playground. And it looked like she wasn't going to freak about anything. "It's Lulu," Alfie said after a couple of silent moments. "Lulu Marino," she added, as if there were several Lulus in her class, and her mom might be confused.

"Lulu Marino," her mother repeated. "Your best friend last year. The 'special darling' with the long straight bangs and all the clothes."

"Outfits," Alfie corrected her. "That's the one. She says her mom makes her lay out everything she's going to wear the next day on her bed each night, to see how it looks. Like she's a big flat paper doll or something."

"I know a gray kitty who would make short work of that little scheme," her mom said, laughing.

"Anyway," Alfie said, "all us girls were friends with each other at the same time—for about one second, I guess. And I wanted things to stay that way. But then on Monday, Lulu said she was gonna have a sleepover this Saturday night. 'Just like the big girls have,' she kept telling us. The best sleepover ever, in fact—but she can only ask a few girls, her mom said. That's when the whispering and the hurt feelings started," she added, her voice fading.

"That's a rule-breaker though, right?" Alfie's mom said. "Talking at school about parties some kids won't be invited to?"

Alfie nodded. "But nobody can tell Mr. Havens about it," she explained to her mom. "Because if we did, Lulu would cut us off her guest list for sure. Besides," she added, frowning, "Mr. Havens doesn't really get girl-stuff, I don't think. You know," she reminded her mom. "Because he's a boy teacher."

"Got it," Mrs. Jakes said. "That is, I don't think you're right, but I hear what you're saying."

"But it's even more complicated than that. Not that I want you to fix anything," Alfie hurried to say before her mom came up with one of her way-too-easy solutions. "Because Lulu says she won't decide who she's inviting until *Friday afternoon*, even though I know I'm not going."

"And just how do you know that?" her mom asked.

"Because I told Lulu in private that she should invite all the girls in our class to her party," Alfie confessed. "I'm not saying where I got *that* bright idea," she added, before her mom could ask. "But Lulu told me to mind my own business. And that I wasn't gonna be invited anymore—for sure."

"Hmm," Alfie's mother said.

"So now Lulu's got everybody all worked up," Alfie said. "And there are only two more days left for her to decide who she's gonna ask. On top of that," she added before she could stop herself, "Mr. Havens knows something is wrong! He made me stay behind at lunch and talk to him."

"You?" her mom asked, surprised. "Why not Lulu?"

"Because he doesn't know what's going on," Alfie explained. "Not exactly. He knows something's wrong, though," she added. "And he says he thinks I'm kind of like a leader of the girls," she added with an it's-not-funny laugh. "But I'm no leader."

She left out the part about her being a bridge. That was just too weird to explain.

"Oh, I wouldn't say that," her mom said, thinking about it.

"I sure would," Alfie said, breaking the news. "Anyway, Mr. Havens wanted me to tell him what was happening with the girls," she added, making a face.

"And did you?" her mom asked.

"No. And there wasn't any time to tell the other girls about what he wanted, either," Alfie said, scootching away from her mom a little as she stretched the truth. She didn't like to fib.

Okay, *lie.*

Maybe there *had* been time to tell the girls,

Alfie admitted to herself. But what was she supposed to say to them? And why stick her neck out now, when she did not have a chance in the world of going to the party?

"Okay, I've heard enough," Alfie's mom said, standing up. "But it's no wonder you've had the yips, sweetie. I think I'd like to go downstairs and talk to your dad about this one."

Her *dad*? But he made everything super-complicated, he was so serious.

"I can't explain it all again, Mom," Alfie argued, faking a gigantic yawn. "I'm already half asleep, and so is Princess. And you told Dad *you* were gonna handle it."

"Yes. But this sounds serious, and I'd like your father's input," her mom said. "You can join us for a conference in the morning, Alfleta. I'll get you up a little earlier."

Alfie groaned. "Okay," she said. "But I don't get how we're gonna conference our way out of this one," she added, struggling to keep her voice calm. "Anyway, I was just trying to explain my *mood* to you, Mom. Not start a battle or anything."

"The three of us will talk about it in the morning," Mrs. Jakes said again. "Now, get some sleep, sweetie."

"Easy for *you* to say," Alfie mumbled into her covers as her mother slipped out the door.

Don't Sweat the Small Stuff

It was strange, Alfie thought early the next morning, Thursday, standing next to her mom in the family room doorway. The room looked almost unfamiliar, as if it woke up a little bit new each day, wondering what might happen next.

She was usually brushing her teeth at this time on a school morning, Alfie thought. Maybe that was it.

"All the way in, Cricket," her dad said, laughing from where he was sitting on the sofa. Alfie's mom showed her where to sit—as if Alfie were a guest in her own home.

"I was telling your dad last night about your difficult week," her mother began.

"Mostly yesterday," Alfie said, trying to get it right. "Yesterday was the worst. And all I wanted was for all the girls in my class to stay friends at the same time."

But then there was seeing Bella cry in the girls' room. Not that Alfie's parents knew about that.

And observing the miffed, hurt, irked, and furious girls in her class.

And having that disastrous talk with Lulu about inviting everyone to her sleepover.

And being late to Social Studies for the first time ever.

And having to stay in class during the first part of lunch, with Mr. Havens trying to get her to tell him what was going on—because she was such a great leader, ha ha.

And then there was her mom coming upstairs to talk about her *mood.*

"It was difficult mostly yesterday," Alfie's father said, repeating her words. "But you know, Alfie, your mother and I attended a parents' meeting a few weeks ago, toward the end of summer. And Principal James was talking about just this sort of thing. He gave us parents some pretty good advice."

Alfie blinked. Her dad was talking about something Principal James had said four weeks ago? She could barely remember what she'd had for dinner last night! And what was "just this sort of thing" supposed to mean?

"But how did Principal James know this was gonna happen?" Alfie asked, frowning. "Is he magic or something?"

"Of course not, sweetie," her mother assured her. "And Principal James didn't know, not exactly. He just warned us that something like this was bound to happen this year. A feud among the girls," she added, explaining.

"Boys fight," Alfie told her parents. She did not like the girls being singled out this way. Four weeks in advance, too—before they'd even done anything wrong!

"What Principal James was telling us was that in most cases, we parents should remain calm and not get involved in any minor squabbles, if possible," her mother said. "It can just make everything worse, he said—unless someone's safety is involved," she added, trying to remember the details of his talk. "Then, parents have to step in, of course. The principal called it a 'No Interference Policy,'" she added, explaining.

"'*Don't sweat the small stuff,*'" Alfie's father said, quoting from the meeting, Alfie guessed.

"And so last night, your father and I had just about decided to try to stay out of the whole thing—even though this doesn't really seem all that small to us. Not with you stuck in the middle," Mrs. Jakes said, patting Alfie on the knee to show her concern. "But then my cell phone started to buzz."

"And now the matter is out of our hands," Alfie's dad said.

Alfie's heart began to thud. "What's that supposed to mean?" she asked. Her dad was so strong! *Especially* his hands.

"It means that some other girls talked to their parents, too," her mother said. "And the All-Stars' phone tree got a real workout last night."

"But what parents?" Alfie asked. "*Whose* parents?"

"Arletty's and Phoebe's, for starters," her father reported.

"Not that it really matters whose parents," Alfie's mom chimed in. "There were a couple of other calls as well, once the ball got rolling. And I assume Lulu's mother got a call or two before the night was over. After all, she's really the one who planned this party in the first place."

"She didn't tell Lulu to blab it all over school," Alfie pointed out. "But what about Lulu's sleepover? Is it still gonna happen?"

"I have no idea," her mom said. "I finally turned off my phone and went to bed."

"But turning off your phone didn't make the problem go away, Mom," Alfie said, her voice shaking. "Lulu's going to blame me for everything!"

"Why you?" her dad asked.

"Because I'm the only one who tried standing up to her," Alfie said. "Only now, I don't really even *care* about the sleepover. I decided last night to just wait for this week to be over, and then hope things would get better for all us girls. That was my big plan—until *this* happened."

"Very wise, too," Mr. Jakes announced, listening to just part of what she said.

"No, wait!" Alfie said to her parents. "What am I supposed to tell Lulu?"

"You don't have to tell her anything," her mother said. "*You* didn't make this happen, Alfie. The other girls' parents did. And most of all, Lulu did. But I do want you to keep us in the loop about what happens next, okay?"

"I'll try," Alfie said. "I mean, if I can remember it all."

Because there was gonna be a ton of stuff, she told herself gloomily.

The Worst Best Sleepover Ever

It was a perfect morning—except for having to go to school, Alfie thought as she waited for Mrs. Sobel to pick her up for carpool half an hour later. Puffy white clouds floated across the sky. Leaves blew down the street as if they were chasing each other.

"Have fun while you can, you guys," Alfie called after them.

Too bad today was gonna be such a disaster, she thought.

Arletty and Phoebe—currently her two best friends at Oak Glen Primary School—were so upset about Lulu's sleepover that they told their parents about it. But they weren't the only ones.

"Hey," Hanni said, greeting Alfie with a funny face as she climbed into Mrs. Sobel's car.

"Hey to you, too," Alfie said, making a face back at her.

Apart from the funny face, Hanni looked perfectly normal. So she hadn't heard about the phone calls yet, Alfie thought.

"Thank goodness," she whispered at school as she got out of the Sobels' car.

❋ ❋ ❋

"There she is," Lulu Marino called out in a cold, hard voice as Alfie and Hanni neared the picnic table where the second grade girls liked to gather before school.

Alfie could feel her heart going down, down, down to her very basement, if a person could even *have* a basement.

"She, who?" Hanni was asking Lulu in a voice that was just as loud. "There are two of us here, you know. Can't you count?"

Wow, Alfie thought, surprised at Hanni's sparky reply. Hanni had guts! She must have totally given up yesterday on being invited to the sleepover. No more kissing-up to Lulu Marino, it seemed.

"I can count better than you, Hanni Sobel," Lulu boasted. "But I was talking to Alfie. And the point *is*," she said, flicking her long bangs as she gave both Hanni and Alfie the stink-eye, "my whole sleepover is ruined because of you, Alfie Jakes."

"Why because of me?" Alfie asked.

"Because Mama started getting these *phone calls* last night," Lulu said. "Because you blabbed when you didn't get your way about who I should ask to my sleepover. So now, Mama says the whole thing is canceled. Period."

"But not because of me," Alfie insisted, not looking at either Arletty or Phoebe, whose parents had made the first calls. "My parents didn't call your mom."

"*Yes,* because of you," Lulu insisted. "You turned my party into the worst best sleepover ever!" she went on. "And now it has *disappeared.* No more party. Thanks a lot."

Unfair, Alfie thought, her face growing hot with embarrassment. She had been going to give up and wait it out! And even her *parents* had decided not to interfere. It was Arletty's and Phoebe's parents who first called her mom's cell last night! And other parents, too. Alfie wasn't about to tell *Lulu* that, though.

But now, all the girls were looking at her.

"Alfie was jealous of my big-girls party," Lulu announced to everyone. "And so she went and ruined it. And now we're all stuck being *kindergarten babies* again. Thanks a lot, Alfie," she repeated, turning her icy glare back in Alfie's direction. "Party pooper," she added, and her eyes narrowed.

Alfie almost giggled, hearing the word "pooper." But she held it together.

"I didn't ruin your party," she finally said.

"Oh, *sure* you didn't," Lulu said, shaking her head. "Like we all believe you!" She turned back to the wide-eyed group. "I think nobody should ask Alfie to a party ever again," she announced. "*All year long.* That should be her punishment. Right, you guys? Because she's such a blabbermouth, and she wrecked my sleepover? The best one ever?"

Nobody said anything.

But now no one would look at Alfie—whose heart was beating hard.

This was the *complete opposite* of her wish for everyone to be—and stay—friends at the same time.

How could things go so wrong in just four measly days?

"So that's settled," Lulu said, brushing her hands together as if getting rid of some pesky dirt. She was acting as if she had just won a huge argument, and the girls were all cheering her on—which they were not. *"Party pooper,"* Lulu said again as she swept past Alfie.

That was it for Alfie. "I don't think you can be a party pooper if the party never happens in the first place," she pointed out in a loud voice. "And don't you have to be there to, um, poop the party?"

Uh-oh, she thought, her mouth starting to twitch. *Don't laugh,* she told herself. That would just make everything worse!

If that was even possible.

But it was too late, because a couple of other girls were already giggling.

And Lulu heard them.

"Like *you* were ever gonna be invited, Alfie Jakes," Lulu said, whirling around. "Stop laughing, you guys!" she yelled, stomping her foot—like a kindergarten baby, Alfie couldn't help but think.

And just like that, she felt sorry for Lulu.

Sure, Lulu had messed up and done something wrong, bragging about her sleepover the way she had.

Making Bella cry.

Hurting other girls' feelings.

Blaming Alfie for no reason.

And then trying to get the other girls to punish her.

But she knew Lulu Marino. And being laughed at was something that Lulu could not stand.

"I'm sorry about your party," Alfie called after Lulu as the angry girl stormed her way across the playground. "Really, Lulu! Because it sounded like the best sleepover ever!"

But Lulu didn't answer.

Ready for a Party

"So, it's over, right?" Alfie's mom asked that Thursday night as she and Alfie were making dinner. Tuesdays and Thursdays were Alfie's evenings to help prepare the meal. EllRay got Mondays and Wednesdays. "Lulu's sleepover has been called off," Mrs. Jakes said, spelling it out. "Things must have started to settle down today."

If you say so, Alfie wanted to tell her mom, though rude comments like that did not fly in her house. They led to family meetings, heart-to-heart talks, and, worst of all, "consequences." Mr. and Mrs. Jakes were big on consequences when their kids did something wrong.

But things had not "settled down" in Mr Havens's

class that day. And Alfie was feeling frazzled.

Lulu still believed that Alfie was the one who had tattled about the sleepover.

And Suzette Monahan was as mad as Lulu that there wasn't going to be a party.

And Phoebe—one of the upset girls whose parents had made last night's phone calls—blushed each time Alfie looked her way.

And Arletty, the other upset girl, was sad that everyone else was sad.

And Bella had been jumpy all day.

"Alfie?" Mrs. Jakes was saying, pausing as she peeled a carrot. "Things settled down today once the sleepover was called off, right?"

"A little," Alfie said from the sink, where she was washing some potatoes. She could not look her mom in the eye. She seemed so hopeful!

But Alfie was determined to keep her "in the loop" a little, at least, the way her mother had asked the night before. Life would just be easier that way, Alfie figured.

Alfie Jakes did not like it when life got tangled-up and complicated.

"Why did things settle down only a little?" her

mom asked, taking a seat at the kitchen island. "Sit down, Alfie. Talk to me."

"But these potatoes—"

"Princess could use a nice warm lap to curl up in," her mother said. "The potatoes can wait. Speak, sweetie," Mrs. Jakes told Alfie.

"Okay," Alfie said, picking up the kitten. "Well, like I thought, Lulu thinks I was the one who told on her and ruined her party," she reported gloomily. "Even though I didn't do it. But nothing is ever gonna change her mind. I think some girls even believe her. Suzette does, for sure. And Lulu told everyone never to invite me to a party again—all year long. So there goes second grade."

"They won't listen to her," Mrs. Jakes said. "They were probably just afraid to say anything."

"But a couple of the girls are mad because they were sure they were going to be invited," Alfie argued as Princess purred in her lap. "So they figure they missed out on one really fun party. 'The best sleepover ever.'"

"What about the other girls in your class?" Mrs. Jakes asked, tilting her head.

"I don't know," Alfie replied as she stared down

at her hands. "Some of them blame me, probably."

Mrs. Jakes considered what Alfie had just told her. "You girls were really ready for a party, it sounds like," she finally said. "I mean, you've been together for a month now, with a new teacher, and that's something to celebrate. So it only makes sense that you were all ready for a good time. *Celebrate the small things*, I always say."

"I guess," Alfie said, thinking about it. "It did sound fun," she admitted to her mom.

"Listen. You know I will do anything I can to help you get through this, don't you, sweetie?" Alfie's mother asked after a few silent moments.

"Mm-hmm," Alfie said, nodding. "Only there's nothing you can do."

"Maybe we can come up with some ideas," her mom suggested.

"We only need *one* idea," Alfie said. "But it would have to be a good one."

"Such as?" Mrs. Jakes asked, leaning forward.

"Well," Alfie said, gazing up at the kitchen ceiling, "I dunno. The only thing that might work would be to have a party anyway. Somewhere else, I mean, because Mrs. Marino says she's not in the mood anymore. But we would absolutely invite every girl in our class," she added, thinking about Bella and some of the others.

"Including Lulu Marino," Alfie's mother said.

"I guess," Alfie said with a sigh. "If she'd come. Except then, Lulu would say I stole her idea," she added, drooping. "And she'd probably be right."

"We might be able to find a way around that," her mother said. "And we could have it here, maybe. It doesn't have to be a sleepover, after all."

"But we couldn't have a party *here*," Alfie pointed out. "We don't have enough room for that many kids."

"I think we could do it in a pinch," her mom said. "How many girls are there in your class? Twelve, altogether? Thirteen?"

Alfie nodded. "Thirteen. But our house isn't as big as Lulu's house," she pointed out. "And Lulu said her house was too small to hold all of us."

"I think we *could* fit everyone in here," her mom said. "It's just a question of doing it—if you'd like to give it a try, that is. It would be crowded, that's for sure. But I think everybody would have fun. Things don't have to be perfect for people to have a good time."

"Thirteen girls?" Alfie said, trying to picture it.

"With you as the host, and Lulu as the honored guest, since since she had the idea first," her mom said. "Whatever kind of party you decide to have. If you'd like to *have* a party, that is." She gave her daughter a searching look.

"Let me think about it," Alfie said. "I'm not really sure."

Lulu Marino as the honored guest? That was going pretty far!

"Okay," her mom said. "But think fast, because tomorrow is Friday, sweetie. So if you want to have the party this Saturday night, I would have to get on the phone by tomorrow afternoon at the latest. Of course, we could always wait a few weeks if you'd prefer," she said, tapping her chin as she thought.

"But everyone's frazzled *now*, Mom," Alfie said. "And you're right—we're ready for a party. We *earned* it."

"I think you have," her mother agreed.

“So, I’ll think about it fast,” Alfie said again. “Okay?”

“Well, keep me in the loop,” Mrs. Jakes said, standing up and stretching.

There was that invisible loop again!

“I will,” Alfie promised. “And thanks, Mom,” she added, giving her mother a surprise hug. “You make me have the best ideas ever!”

“High praise indeed,” Mrs. Jakes said, smiling. “Now, let’s get back to fixing dinner.”

16

Upside-Down Heads

"We gotta talk, Lulu. *Alone,*" Alfie said just before lunch the next day, Friday, when Writing Workshop was over. Stories that had beginnings, middles, and ends—however hastily tacked on—had been piled up on Mr. Havens's desk, and the All-Stars were rushing to the cubby room for their lunches.

Stomachs were growling.

A jumble of noise—excited chatter, and Scooter Davis's and Bryan Martinez's frantic yelps—provided an invisible curtain of privacy as she spoke.

"Why? So you can lie to me again about not wrecking my party?" Lulu asked, sounding almost bored. "There's no hope of making it right now, Alfie. So why bother?"

"Because we used to be friends," Alfie whisper-shouted. "So it's important. Let's meet in the cafeteria, okay? Because everyone else will be eating outside at the picnic tables."

"Okay," Lulu said, shrugging. "Who cares?"

She'd been like that all morning, even at recess. Lulu was drooping like one of the weed flowers Alfie used gather into scrubby bouquets for her mom.

Those flowers never lasted very long in her small hot hands.

But droopy was better than angry any day of the week, Alfie reminded herself, losing sight of Lulu in the crowded hallway.

❋ ❋ ❋

The Oak Glen Primary School cafeteria came with its own invisible curtain of noise—and with soapy, greasy smells as well. Alfie spotted Lulu sitting alone at the end of a long beige formica table. She was arranging her lunch in front of her as if she were going to try to paint a picture of it, not eat it, Alfie thought.

Poor Lulu.

Poor *mean* Lulu, Alfie reminded herself sternly, recalling the way Lulu had acted all week—especially when she'd made Bella cry.

But Lulu wasn't mean, not usually, Alfie thought. She remembered the long and happy first grade playdates they'd had together—playing with dolls, making their own playdough, telling stories, building fancy LEGO castles, watching cartoons—and playing "Upside-Down Heads."

Their heads really did seem upside-down now, things were so messed up.

But just the thought of all that fun they'd had gave Alfie some of the confidence she knew she was going to need for this conversation. "Hey," she said, slipping into the chair across from Lulu and reaching into her own lunch bag with pretend enthusiasm.

She was hungry, but could she eat?

"Hey," Lulu replied, reaching for her sandwich. "What did you want to talk about?" She was starting to sound a little interested, in spite of herself.

"I'm really sorry about your sleepover, Lulu," Alfie began, examining her own sandwich with exaggerated care. "Only I didn't ruin it," she added, repeating the words she'd spoken the day before. "I wanted to go, in fact," she said, deciding to tell the truth.

"And I wanted you to come," Lulu said, as if she were admitting something, too.

"So, what happened?" Alfie asked, her brown eyes wide.

"When Mama and I got the idea for the sleepover," Lulu tried to explain, "she came up with all these rules, see. You know how she gets."

"I guess I do," Alfie said, not looking at Lulu. But she'd had lots of playdates at Lulu's house last year, so she *did* know how Mrs. Marino could be at times.

Way too much in Lulu's business, in Alfie's opinion. Every little thing!

How long Lulu had to brush her teeth.

How much money she had to save from her allowance each week.

"In her grill," as Alfie's big brother EllRay might say, pretending to be tough.

Maybe Mrs. Marino was like that because Lulu was an only child, Alfie told herself now. Who knew? Lulu was kind of like her mother's main job, Alfie thought—and her hobby too, for that matter.

Think of all Lulu's super-cute outfits, for instance.

And her bangs, always so perfectly trimmed.

Things like that took time.

And it was a lot of responsibility for Lulu, Alfie thought. She felt sorry for her. Almost.

"See, last summer was hard," Lulu was trying to explain.

Alfie blinked, wanting to keep up. "You mean in *Maine*?" she asked, surprised. Lulu and her parents had been gone the whole summer, she remembered. It had been the longest vacation in the world, as far as Alfie was concerned. "Why? Wasn't it fun? It sounded fun."

"It was fun being with my grandparents," Lulu said. "Only I didn't have anyone much to play with, either."

"What about your cousins?" Alfie asked. "I thought you had tons."

"They're older," Lulu said, her voice soft with leftover sadness. "The point *is,* they've been friends with each other since forever. So Mama and I were kind of lonely on that island," she said, poking a hole through what was left of her sandwich.

"Huh," Alfie said, thinking about it.

"I would have video-called you," Lulu continued, "only I couldn't get a signal."

Wow, Alfie thought—but it was an island! *She* would have had fun. She wondered if any mermaids swam nearby—if mermaids were real. She could never decide about that.

But she would have left out snacks for them, just in case.

"So when we got back," Lulu was saying, "Mama told me it was time for us to have some fun. And so we decided it would be a good time to have a sleepover. I partly wanted to do it for my mama," Lulu confided, like this was a secret. "She likes to plan stuff so much. That's why her feelings were hurt on Wednesday night, when she started getting those phone calls saying how wrong she was about the party."

"But didn't your mom know about the school rule?" Alfie asked.

"*She* didn't break the rule," Lulu reminded her. "*I* did. I guess I kind of got carried away with the whole thing, once I saw how much everyone wanted to go to my party."

"Uh-huh," Alfie said, nodding. "I kind of get that. But how come you had to go and make Bella cry the way you did?"

"I didn't *have* to," Lulu admitted. "But I wanted to—when I saw her in the restroom that day. She kind of made me feel bad, looking so sad and lonely. And that made me *mad* for some reason. I don't know why," she added with a tiny shrug. "Just like I don't know why I said you weren't my friend anymore," she added softly, looking away.

Alfie held her breath.

Even

"I'm sorry I said you weren't my friend anymore," Lulu said again.

In front of everyone, Alfie added silently. "Oh, did you say that?" she asked out loud, kicking the cafeteria chair with her sneaker. "I guess I didn't hear."

"Yeah, you did," Lulu said, laughing. "But the point *is*, I didn't mean it. So do you forgive me?"

"You meant it a little bit," Alfie said, her voice quiet. "For a second, at least."

"But being mad at someone for a second doesn't count," Lulu said. "Not for Upside-Down Heads like us," she added, and she slid Alfie a pleading look.

"Why did you say it?" Alfie asked as she remembered the awful moment.

"Like I said before, I got carried away," Lulu said.

"Well, can you quit getting carried away?" Alfie asked, only half joking.

"I can try," Lulu said.

"Okay, then," Alfie said. "But getting back to before, I think your cousins not wanting to play with you should have made you want to be *nice* to Bella."

"But it didn't," Lulu said, frowning a little. "So, okay, I yelled at Bella for no reason. And I guess I'm sorry."

"Tell Bella that," Alfie said. "And then we'll be even."

"Okay. *Maybe*," Lulu said as she opened a small bag of grapes and popped one into her mouth. "But how come you want that so much?"

"Because it's the nice thing to do," Alfie said. "Just like it would have been nice if your cousins played with you last summer."

"And not kept ditching me," Lulu chimed in. "On an *island*. Like, who was I supposed to play with? The rocks? And it kept raining!"

"So, tell Bella you're sorry," Alfie said again.

"Okay, okay," Lulu said with a dramatic sigh. "I'll *apologize.* I promise. But we're still stuck with no party," she added, scooping her lunch trash back into its crumpled brown paper bag.

"Maybe we are, and maybe we aren't," Alfie said, thinking.

"What's that supposed to mean?" Lulu asked.

And Alfie told her the basic idea.

"So let me get this straight," Lulu Marino said a few minutes later. "You want to have a party tomorrow—at your house? And invite all the girls in our class?"

Alfie nodded. "Because that was such a great idea you had," she told Lulu.

"And that's why you would be, like, the honored guest at the party," Alfie went on.

"Really?" Lulu asked.

"Mm-hmm," Alfie said, nodding some more. "But I wanted to check it out with you first."

"What kind of party?" Lulu asked. She was starting to get excited.

"I dunno yet," Alfie admitted.

"Not a sleepover," Lulu said. "Because I want to be the first one in our class to have a sleepover—like the big girls have."

"Okay," Alfie agreed. "But what else sounds like fun?"

Lulu shrugged. "I don't know. Maybe something kinda *like* a sleepover," she said slowly. "A party where you get to wear your cutest jammies. And then just eat something and go home."

"Yeah," Alfie said, picturing it. "The girls could *come* wearing their awesomest jammies. And eat breakfast, maybe. With no sleeping over."

"Because breakfast is my most favorite meal of the day," Lulu said, rubbing her stomach.

"Chocolate chip pancakes," Alfie said, remembering her old friend's favorites. "Or breakfast burritos. Or toaster waffles."

"Or all three," Lulu said, laughing. "Let's have everything! And *games*."

"We can call it the 'Jammie Breakfast Party,'" Alfie suggested.

"Or the 'Saturday Morning Jammie Breakfast Party,'" Lulu said. "So the girls know exactly when they're supposed to come. Because we're talking about *tomorrow morning,* Alfie."

Jeesh, Alfie thought, her eyes wide with alarm. She'd better call her mom!

The school office lady would let her use the phone, she was pretty sure.

"Let's go outside and invite all the other girls, before lunch is over," Lulu was saying.

"You do it," Alfie said. "Because I have to run to the office and call my mom, or our Saturday Morning Jammie Breakfast Party is never gonna happen."

"Go," Lulu shouted. "Go!"

The Saturday Morning Jammie Breakfast Party!

"What did I ever do to deserve this?" EllRay asked early the next morning, pausing before blowing up more balloons.

It was almost time for the Saturday Morning Jammie Breakfast Party!

"You got to have me as a little sister, that's what happened," Alfie said, almost dancing, she was so excited. "Do you like my new jammies?" she asked, twirling in front of him.

"*I* do," Lulu Marino said. She had arrived early—to make sure she was there when the first guest arrived, and to help a little. Lulu had decided to wear a long gauzy skirt and a sparkly top to the breakfast party. Her shiny black hair even had some glitter in it. "I mean, it's what I sleep in," she had claimed, adjusting the frothy layers of her skirt.

"I *guess* I like your jammies," EllRay said, giving his sister the once-over. "But they're more like leggings and a big T-shirt, if you ask me."

"Cute, though," Alfie added, admiring herself the best that she could. Her new jammie bottoms were striped, and the top was covered with large, colorful flowers. "I feel like a bumblebee," she said, totally satisfied.

The entire Jakes family had sprung into action the night before, piling into Mrs. Jakes' car right after dinner.

They shopped first at the party store for decorations and favors.

Then Alfie and her mom dashed into a department store to score Alfie's awesome new jammies.

Then they cruised the supermarket aisles for a cartful of breakfast fixings.

They ended the night at the bakery counter, picking up the special cake Alfie's mom had ordered the afternoon before, after Alfie called from the office. *Good Morning, All-Star Girls!* was spelled out on top of the cake. It was decorated with thirteen roses, and the cheerful message made Alfie happy each time she looked at it.

Now Princess was safely stashed away in her parents' bedroom so she couldn't slip out the front door as guests came and went. Music was already playing. And the savory scent of fried sausage—for the breakfast burritos to come—wafted into the living room.

"Are you gonna wear those sweatpants and basketball team shirt and saggy socks to the party?" Lulu asked EllRay, who had started blowing up more balloons.

"I'm not gonna be *at* the party," EllRay informed her, pinching the end of a half-inflated balloon as he paused to answer her question. "Me and my dad are going out for, like, a *year,* I think we decided," he added, shooting Alfie a look.

Sque-e-eak! went the balloon as EllRay let out a little air.

"Send me postcards," Alfie said, her hands over her ears.

"Me too, okay?" Lulu said, fluffing up her skirt again. "Because I don't have a brother."

She was clearly awed by being in the presence of a sixth-grader, Alfie thought. Even if it was only EllRay.

EllRay darted Alfie a second look, this one

saying, *Get her away from me!* because honored guest Lulu Marino's antics were making Suzette Monahan's old McDonald's demand look like nothing, Alfie thought, trying not to laugh.

First, Lulu had insisted on peeking inside all the already-wrapped party favors.

Then she'd tasted the frosting on the cake and sampled the crumbled sausage.

She'd even wandered into Dr. Jakes' home office without permission.

Her dad would be talking about "pulling a Lulu" from now on whenever someone acted up, Alfie was sure.

But she and Lulu were good again.

"Who's coming, did you say?" Lulu asked Alfie.

"I already told you twice," Alfie said, peeking out the living room window. "Everyone except two new girls whose families already had plans."

"So that makes nine other kids," Lulu said, nodding.

"Including Arletty," Alfie said, happy that her old friend could make it to the morning party after all. "And Bella, don't forget," she added, and she turned to look at Lulu.

"I already said 'Sorry,' don't worry," Lulu told her, laughing.

"I think your first guests have arrived, ladies," Mrs. Jakes said, nodding toward the front door as she walked into the room. "So let's have a party!"

But Alfie and Lulu held back as Mrs. Jakes headed for the door. There were butterflies fluttering around inside her tummy, Alfie thought, rubbing it. She could not imagine how Lulu was feeling. "Are you happy?" she asked her old friend.

"Mostly," Lulu said, her voice soft. "I was thinking about my sleepover for a second, that's all."

"It would've been great," Alfie said. "But this isn't a sleepover, Lulu. And you can still have your party someday. So why be sad when you're about to be happy?"

Lulu suddenly looked lost. "I don't *know,*" she said, her eyes wide.

And Alfie believed her. Maybe feeling always a little bit sad was a "special darling" thing, she figured, because—how perfect could things be most of the time?

But things were cool enough anyway.

The sound of excited voices floated in from the front door.

"I'm glad you're here," Alfie told Lulu.

"Really?" Lulu asked.

"Really."

"I am, too," Lulu said, brightening.

Her smile was sunny now, and Alfie smiled back at her. "Let's have a party," she said, echoing her mom's earlier words.

"Okay," Lulu said. She reached for Alfie's hand, and Alfie's heart gave a jump of pure happiness.

Freeze!

Don't forget to look out
for other books
featuring

ABSOLUTELY
Alfie

ABSOLUTELY

Alfie

• and the •

FURRY PURRY SECRET

by

SALLY WARNER

illustrated by

SHEARRY MALONE

ABSOLUTELY Alfie and the FURRY PURRY SECRET

* * *

Alfie Jakes has had a great summer. She went to day camp. She took tumbling *and* swimming lessons. But now that there are just a few weeks left before school starts, her mother decides that Alfie should have playdates with their next-door neighbor. Hanni is in the same grade as Alfie, but she's *bossy*! So at first, Alfie is less than thrilled. Hanni likes to be a know-it-all, but she's also great at sharing. And then she shows Alfie the most wonderful thing ever. A basket full of kittens!

When Hanni hands her the littlest gray kitty, Alfie knows she's in love. Hanni even says she can take it home! Alfie wants to say yes so badly. There's only one problem: a Jakes family rule is **NO PETS!** because she used to be allergic. Alfie is left with no choice. She *must* prove once and for all that her allergies are really, truly, seriously gone. But that could mean keeping secrets from her family and Hanni. Will Operation Kittycat be a success—or will it be a *cat*astrophe??

ABSOLUTELY Alfie

and the FIRST WEEK FRIENDS

by SALLY WARNER

illustrated by SHEARRY MALONE

ABSOLUTELY Alfie
and the
FIRST WEEK FRIENDS

* * *

Alfie Jakes is excited to start second grade. Her new backpack is the cutest. Her outfit has been ready for days. And even though her best friend Lulu was gone most of the summer, Alfie has made friends with another classmate, her neighbor Hanni. But for some reason, Alfie's getting a case of first day jitters. Is it because her teacher is a "boy" and some kids call him Coach?

It's a good thing she will start school with not just one, but two best friends! The three girls can look out for each other. Lulu and Hanni barely know each other, though. And Hanni can be kind of bossy, while Lulu likes to be the center of attention. What if they don't get along, when Alfie's secret second grade wish is for them to become first week friends?

Or what if Alfie's wish comes true—but with a twist she didn't see coming?